Chicks and Salsa

Chicks and Salsa

BY

Aaron Reynolds

ILLUSTRATED BY

Paulette Bogan

SCHOLASTIC INC.
New York Toronto London Auckland Sydney
Mexico City New Delhi Hong Kong Buenos Aires

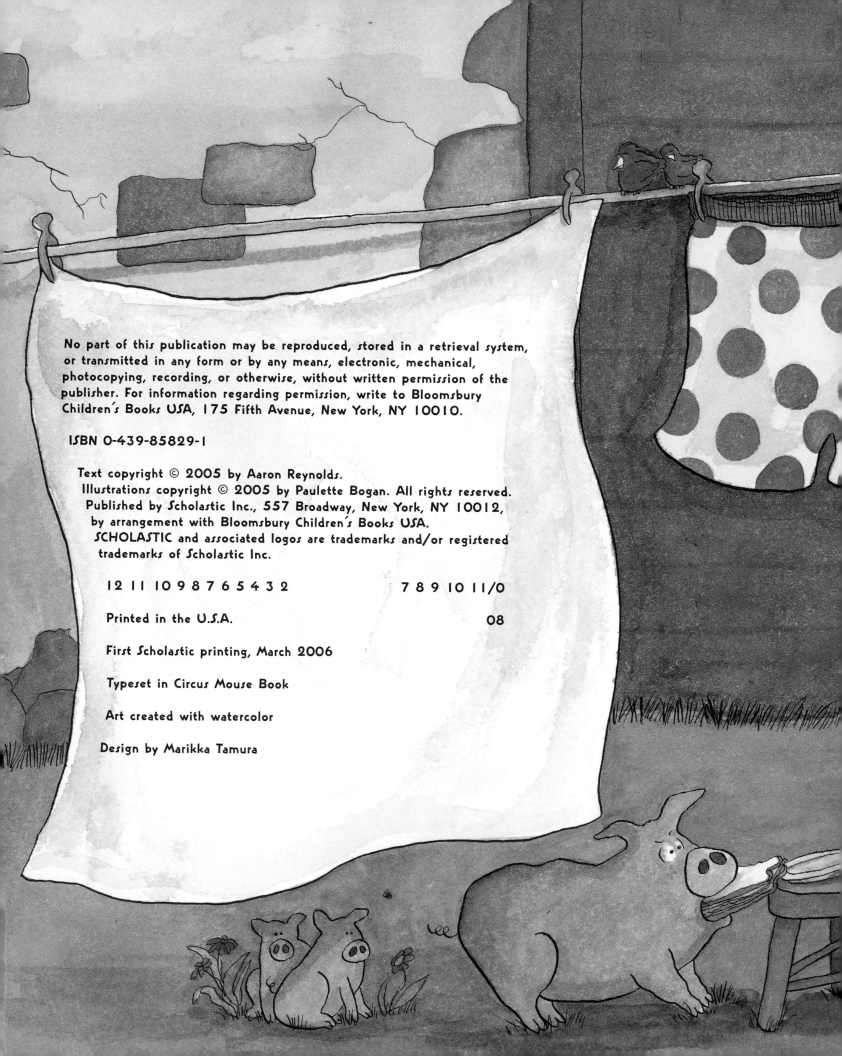

ISBN 0-439-85829-1

Text copyright © 2005 by Aaron Reynolds.
Illustrations copyright © 2005 by Paulette Bogan. All rights reserved.
Published by Scholastic Inc., 557 Broadway, New York, NY 10012,
by arrangement with Bloomsbury Children's Books USA.
SCHOLASTIC and associated logos are trademarks and/or registered
trademarks of Scholastic Inc.

12 11 10 9 8 7 6 5 4 3 2   7 8 9 10 11/0

Printed in the U.S.A.   08

First Scholastic printing, March 2006

Typeset in Circus Mouse Book

Art created with watercolor

Design by Marikka Tamura

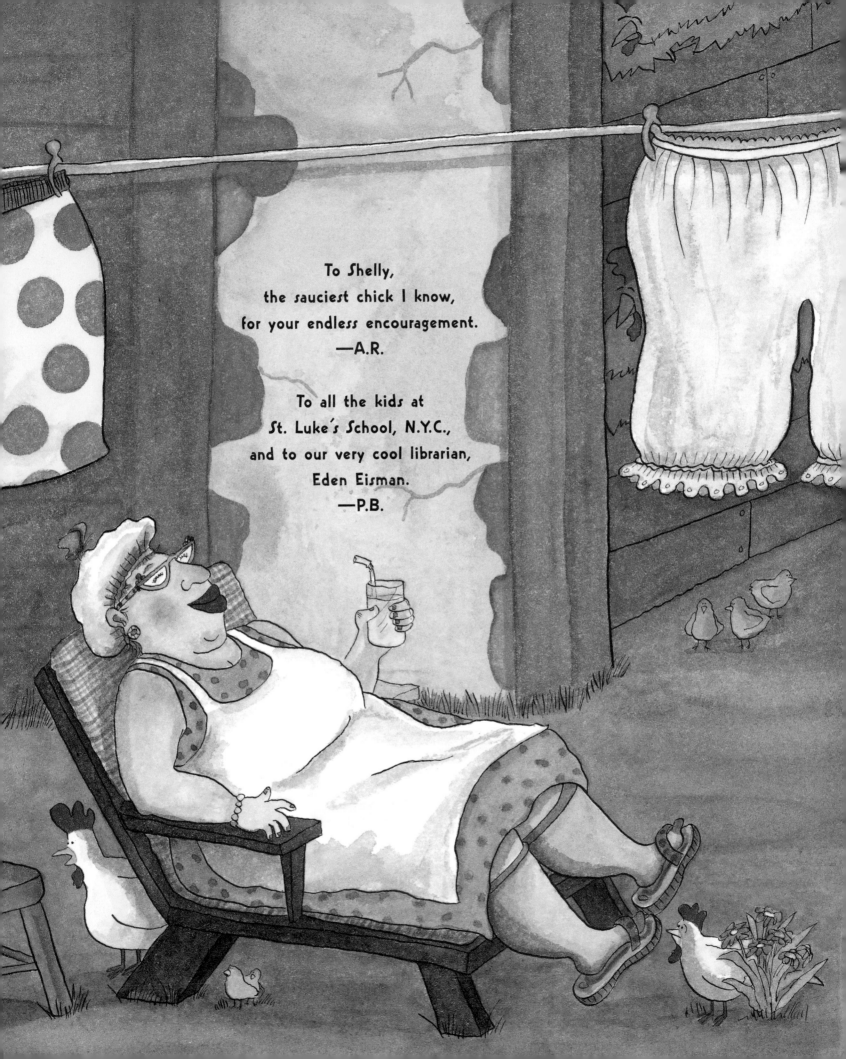

To Shelly,
the sauciest chick I know,
for your endless encouragement.
—A.R.

To all the kids at
St. Luke's School, N.Y.C.,
and to our very cool librarian,
Eden Eisman.
—P.B.

There were grumblings in the henhouse of Nuthatcher
Farm. The chickens were tired of chicken feed.
The rooster took it upon himself to solve this problem.

Mrs. Nuthatcher, the farmer's wife, had started watching cooking shows in the afternoons. The rooster was perched on a fence post outside the farmhouse window when he discovered the solution to his problem . . .

Led by the rooster, the chickens crept into the garden,
where they took tomatoes and uprooted onions.

That night, the chickens ate chips and salsa—
though nobody was quite certain where
the chickens got the chips.

The tasty tang of tomatoes and onions hung over the barnyard.
And the rooster said, "Olé!"

Very soon, there were mumblings at the duck pond of Nuthatcher Farm. Inspired by the chickens, the ducks decided they were tired of fish.

    With the rooster's encouragement, the ducks dipped into the garden, where they selected cilantro and gathered garlic.

That night the ducks ate guacamole—though nobody was quite certain where the ducks got the avocados.

The spicy scent of garlic and cilantro
hung over the barnyard.
And the ducks said, "**Olé!**"

The next morning, there were rumblings in the pigpen of Nuthatcher Farm. Overwhelmed by the enticing aromas, the pigs decided they were tired of slop.

While the rooster distracted Farmer Nuthatcher, the pigs plodded into the garden, where they borrowed beans and chopped chiles.

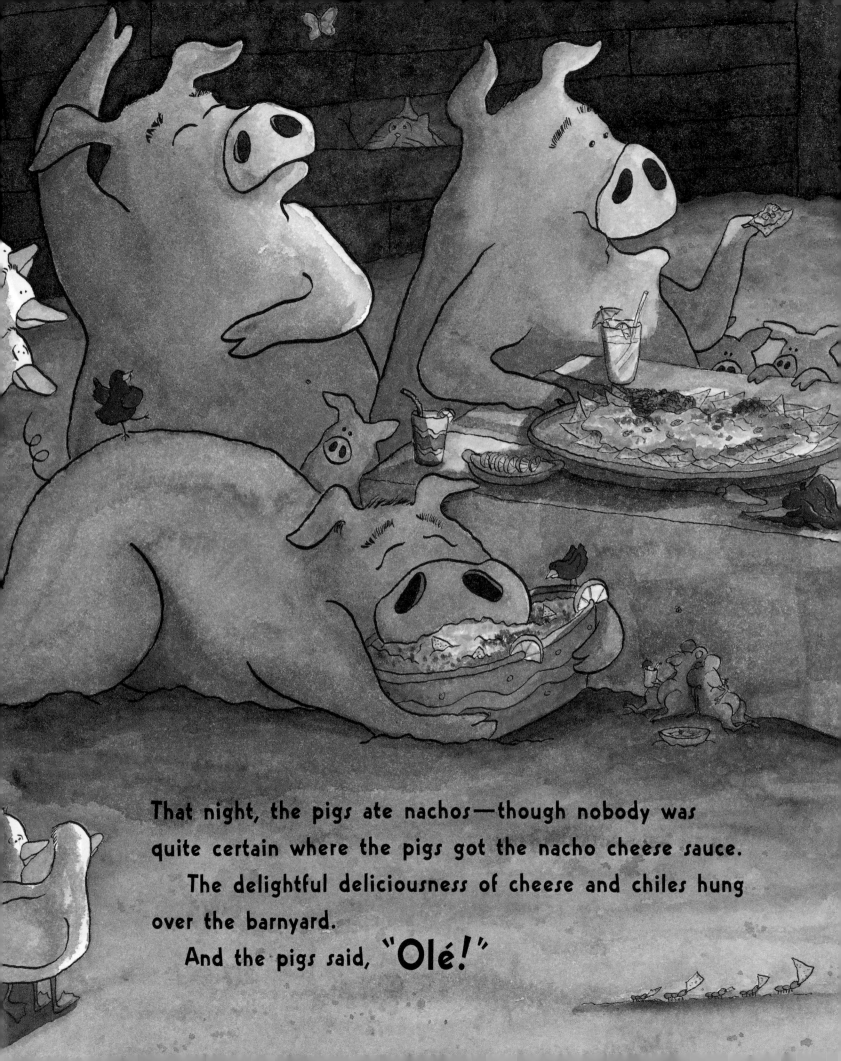

That night, the pigs ate nachos—though nobody was quite certain where the pigs got the nacho cheese sauce.

The delightful deliciousness of cheese and chiles hung over the barnyard.

And the pigs said, "Olé!"

As everyone knows, when a passion for southwestern cuisine takes hold of farm animals, and so many sumptuous, spicy, savory scents collide in the barnyard air, it can only lead to one thing . . .

FIESTA!

The rooster got things organized, then returned to his fence post to watch for a good enchilada recipe. The horses decorated the barn.

The bull practiced his Mexican hat dance—though nobody was quite certain where the bull got the sombrero.

And the chickens, ducks, and pigs snuck into the garden.
But all of their spicy southwestern supplies were gone!

The scallions had been stolen!
The peppers had been pilfered!
The limes had been lifted!

But there were slurpings in the kitchen of Nuthatcher Farm. Stirred by the succulent smells in the barnyard, Mrs. Nuthatcher had decided to make tamales for the county fair.

A saucy sweetness hung over the farmhouse kitchen.
And Mrs. Nuthatcher said, "Olé!"

Disappointed, the animals canceled the fiesta.

That evening the chickens ate their chicken feed,
the ducks ate their fish, and the pigs ate their slop.

But while the Nuthatchers were at the fair, the rooster crept into the kitchen and borrowed a French cookbook. The next morning, the rooster ate crêpes with white grapes in champagne sauce.

Though nobody was quite certain where the rooster learned how to read.

A satisfied smile stretched over the rooster's beak.
And the rooster said, "Ooh la la!"

HOG WILD NACHOS

1 bag tortilla chips
2 cups black beans
1/4 cup chopped green chiles
(substitute fresh jalapeños if you like to go red in the face)
1/4 cup chopped green onions
2 cups nacho cheese sauce
4 tablespoons Rooster's Roasted Salsa
4 tablespoons Quackamole
4 tablespoons sour cream

Spread tortilla chips on a nice platter or in a trough.
Cover with black beans, chiles, and green onions.
Pour nacho cheese sauce over all, then heat in the microwave.
Wipe telltale hoofprints off the microwave door.
Dollop salsa, Quackamole, and sour cream over the top.
Dig in, but don't be a hog—
these really stick to your spareribs!

Kids, have an adult lend a hand before you

QUACKAMOLE

2 green onions
small handful cilantro
1 garlic clove
2 ripe avocados
the juice of 2 limes
2 tablespoons Rooster's Roasted Salsa
½ teaspoon salt or more to taste
a couple dashes hot sauce or red chile sauce

Chop green onions, cilantro, and garlic, and set aside in a bowl.
Halve, peel, and pit avocados, then slice into small pieces and add to bowl.
Add lime juice, salsa, salt, and hot sauce.
Mash with a fork until mixed but not mushy!
You can also use a food processor to mix the ingredients.
Just ask a grown-up to help.

ROOSTER'S ROASTED SALSA

5 plum tomatoes
1 onion
2 tablespoons oil
small handful cilantro
3 garlic cloves
the juice of 1 lime
salt and pepper to taste

Place grill outside the henhouse and preheat.
Cut tomatoes in half. Peel onion and cut in half.
Toss tomatoes and onion with oil in a large bowl.
When grill is hot, roast tomatoes and onion until charred.
Remove tomatoes and onion, roughly chop, and return to bowl with oil. Chop cilantro and garlic.
Add to a small bowl with lime juice.
Mix everything in the large bowl together and add salt and pepper to taste.
Grab a chip! Crow and dip!

art making hay in the kitchen!